THE PRANK

ASHLEY RAE HARRIS

NIGHT FALL

THE PRANK

ASHLEY RAE HARRIS

MINNEAPOLIS

Darby Creek
A division of Lerner Publishing Group, Inc.
241 First Avenue North
Minneapolis, MN 55401 U.S.A.

Website address: www.lernerbooks.com

Cover photograph © Drx/Dreamstime.com.

Main body text set in Memento Regular 12/16.

Library of Congress Cataloging-in-Publication Data
Harris, Ashley Rae.
The prank / by Ashley Rae Harris.
p.   cm. — (Night fall)
Summary: Bridgewater High junior Jordan, eager to fit in with a popular
crowd, takes part in a series of pranks that go horribly wrong, and as she
and her friend Charlie investigate, they begin to wonder if the spirit of a
prank victim who died twenty years earlier is to blame.
ISBN 978-0-7613-7747-4 (lib. bdg. : alk. paper)
[1. Practical jokes—Fiction. 2. Popularity—Fiction. 3. Ghosts—Fiction.
4. Haunted schools—Fiction. 5. High schools—Fiction.
6. Schools—Fiction. 7. Horror stories.] I. Title.
PZ7.H2406Pr 2011
[Fic]—dc22   2011001025

Manufactured in the United States of America
1—BP—7/15/11

To my best friend, who always has my back

Deep into that darkness peering, long I stood there wondering, fearing,
Doubting, dreaming dreams no mortal ever dared to dream before

—*Edgar Allan Poe,* The Raven

ordan made her way to school, taking in the crisp fall morning. She loved biking when the weather was like this—warm enough to go without a jacket, but not hot enough to make her sweat. It was a two-mile ride to Bridgewater High through the center of town. Jordan turned up her iPod as she passed the Chowder Hut. The restaurant was empty now, but she knew as soon as school let out it would be filled with kids laughing and gossiping.

Jordan wondered if Charlie would be there. She thought about his intense brown eyes and the shaggy hair that brushed past the collar on his soccer jersey. There was something about his look, like he didn't care about the way others saw him, that made him irresistible.

Jordan had had a crush on Charlie for more than a year now, but they'd never said more than a few words to each other. Now that Jordan was a junior, she hoped he might pay more attention to her. But he was always hanging around Briony McCormick. Briony was a senior like Charlie and super pretty. She was OK enough, but there was something about her that Jordan didn't quite trust—like she was just a little too perfect. Shiny hair, bright white teeth, matching cardigan, and miniskirt perfect. Jordan herself was more of the worn-in jeans and baggy sweater type.

When Jordan arrived at school, everyone seemed to be running around. The homecoming football game was that Friday, and there were activities to celebrate all week long. The cafeteria was serving cookies decorated in the school colors, and Wednesday was a special pajama day. If this year was anything like the last one, even the teachers would join in the week's festivities and turn a blind eye to the predictable school pranks.

As Jordan approached her locker, she spotted her best friend, Kit. Jordan watched as Kit was nearly knocked over by a group of giggling senior girls in leggings and face paint.

"Whoa, I thought you were going to take a nosedive!" Jordan commented once her friend regained balance.

Kit rolled her eyes as she pulled her shoulder-length brown hair into a sloppy ponytail. "I hate homecoming. It's like all of a sudden everyone is so stoked to be at school just because they're allowed to paint blue stripes on their cheeks. Why can't we just go back to last week, when everyone hated everything?"

"Hey, speak for yourself! We're watching *telenovelas* in Spanish today," Jordan said.

"Whatever. I'd rather be anywhere but at that game."

Jordan sighed and swung an arm around Kit's shoulder. Kit had been her best friend since fourth grade. She usually made Jordan laugh, but sometimes she could be such a downer. Jordan actually *wanted* to go to the game and see Bridgewater High trample St. Philomena's. But then there was the dance afterwards . . .

Jordan had never actually had a date to a school dance. She'd gone to dance parties for Halloween and other casual events, in groups or with Kit, if she could drag her along. But she'd never worn a dress and been picked up by a guy for a formal. It looked like this homecoming would be no different.

Jordan was deep in thought when she came face-to-face with Briony McCormick emerging from the bathroom. Jordan was sure Briony had no idea who she was, so it surprised her when Briony smiled sweetly and said, "Hi, Jordan."

"Oh, hey," Jordan said.

"Cute sweater."

"Um, thanks. It's really old," Jordan stammered.

Briony gave her a tight smile before heading out the door. Jordan looked down at her sweater. She'd taken it from an old trunk of her father's college clothes when her parents were cleaning out the attic. She doubted Briony actually found it cute—in fact, she wondered if there was something more to Briony's compliment. But she couldn't help feeling flattered anyway.

After last period, it was time for "Bridgewater Live" in the gym—a goofy talent show the seniors put on every year. Kit refused to go, of course, and headed home. She invited Jordan to come over once it was through. Since none of teachers seemed to be assigning homework and Halloween was coming up, they had plans to watch some old horror movies later that night.

Jordan found a spot on one of the bleachers toward the back. She sat behind a group of freshmen who were laughing and pulling each other's hair. One of them squirmed to free herself from the grip on her ponytail and accidentally elbowed Jordan. *Maybe Kit had the right idea*, Jordan thought.

She wasn't sure what a talent show had to do with football. She guessed that the point was really to announce the homecoming nominations. The emcee was Bart Tompkins, a gawky senior. Everyone seemed to like him, even though he wasn't considered particularly hot or cool. Wearing a full three-piece suit, Bart started things off with a chicken dance that made the crowd roar with laughter. Then he announced that afternoon's entertainment.

A rock band played a few original songs before shifting into a faster, semi-screaming version of the school anthem, "Onward Knights of Bridgewater." Jordan couldn't tell if they were mocking school spirit or celebrating it. A group of senior girls in strapless spandex tops did a dance routine to "Poker Face," except they'd changed the lyrics to reference Bridgewater High and various members of the football team. They weren't very good, but everyone cheered and screamed anyway.

Bart grabbed the microphone again. "Thank you, lovely senioritas of Bridgewater High. I hope you'll save a dance for me on Friday." The crowd snickered, and the dancers blew exaggerated kisses at the emcee. "And now, what we've all been waiting for: the nominations for this year's homecoming court!"

The various nominees paraded in front of the whooping crowd. Predictably, Briony and Charlie were nominated for homecoming queen and king. Jordan cringed when she saw Charlie offer his arm to escort Briony. Briony beamed up at him. Her hair shone under the fluorescent lighting. Jordan had to admit, they looked kind of great together. As far as she knew, they weren't dating. But it was probably only a matter of time before they started.

All of a sudden, something came flying from the side door and burst with a splash on the gym floor. Briony stumbled slightly, trying to avoid it. Her face twisted into an embarrassed grimace. "What the—?"

Briony bent down to pick up the broken water balloon. It was maroon—the color St. Philomena's team.

"Very funny!" she called out into the crowd, shaking her head with a little laugh. But she looked more annoyed than amused.

Jordan craned her head to see the commotion by the side door, but the freshmen were in her way again. She heard laughter and the footsteps of people running away from where the balloon had been launched. With the mood somewhat spoiled, the emcee quickly finished up the nominations. Principal Weston took the mic and excused everyone.

As she headed out, Jordan stole one last glance at the stage. Briony stood shaking her head and stomping her foot in anger. Charlie was holding her gently by both shoulders and talking softly to her, like he was trying to calm her down. *She's so weird*, Jordan thought for the second time that day.

By the time Jordan got to Kit's, she was ready for a break from the homecoming festivities. Kit was prepared with their favorite oink-out, movie-watching snacks: nachos, cherry soda, and ice cream sandwiches.

"So what should we watch first? Cheerleaders getting axed or zombies on fire?" Kit asked dryly.

"Cheerleaders." They both answered at the same time. Jordan loved hanging out at Kit's. They had the entire basement to themselves.

Kit often complained about her parents' constant arguing, but whenever Jordan was there it seemed like no one was around to bug them.

The house was eerily silent when Jordan crept upstairs to get more ice cream sandwiches. She stood in the dim kitchen, noticing the stillness.

"Boo!"

Jordan jumped a full foot.

"Ha! Scared you!" Kit said from the shadows of the basement doorway.

"You jerk!" Jordan threw one of the ice cream sandwiches at her.

"Well, what do you expect? Just standing there in the dark—too easy!" Kit said, laughing. "C'mon, let's finish *Cheerleader Slasher*."

In the movie, all the cheerleaders started to drop off one by one. Everyone thought the town's creepy librarian was the killer until they finally discovered that the head cheerleader was actually the one murdering everyone. In the final, bloody scene, the football captain wrestled an axe away from the cheerleader in self-defense and accidentally plunged it into

.

her stomach, killing her instantly.

"Women always get screwed in the end," was Kit's final assessment.

"Seriously," Jordan said, "What do you think Mr. Brown would say about this?" Mr. Brown was their creative-writing teacher. He was always trying to get them to think about how women and men are portrayed differently in novels and film.

"He'd probably tell that jock to go jump off a cliff," Kit replied, yawning. "And tell me to go to bed."

"Alright," Jordan said, taking the hint that it was time to head home. "I'll see you tomorrow. Don't let any pom-poms suffocate you while you sleep."

The next day at school, the hallways were buzzing with students trying to figure out who'd thrown the water balloon during the homecoming nominations. A few kids claimed it was students from St. Philomena's. Others said it was just a couple freshmen trying to be cool.

Jordan didn't care much either way. She'd been secretly amused to see Briony get so rattled. During lunch she sat with Kit, who chomped on a turkey sandwich as she brainstormed a new ending for *Cheerleader Slasher*.

"What if after he stabbed her and left her for dead, there was a final shot where her eyes popped back open and she smiled that creepy cheerleader smile?" Kit suggested.

"Well, it would definitely set the stage for the sequel," Jordan agreed.

"Hey, Jordan!" Briony's voice was behind her. Jordan swiveled around.

"Hi, Briony," she answered, surprised.

"We're all going to the Chowder Hut after school. Do you want to come?" Briony said, smiling.

"Um, sure . . ."

"Cool. See you later!" Briony sang as she skipped off, her blonde ponytail swinging with each step.

"Well, that was a shocker. You're going to the Chowder Hut with Briony McCormick?" Kit laughed. "I wonder why she didn't invite me."

Jordan didn't like Kit's tone. She wanted to say, "Maybe she didn't invite you because you always think you're too good for everything." But even as she thought it, she knew it wasn't totally fair. After all, earlier that day she'd been laughing to herself at Briony's misfortune during the homecoming nominations. It wasn't like the two of them were the best of friends. It was a little weird that she was invited.

Could there be any possibility that Charlie liked her after all? That he had asked Briony to include her? Or was it just a coincidence? Jordan had no idea, but she was excited to find out. As much as she tried, she could hardly concentrate on Kit's newest version of the horror film ending.

As she was locking up her bike, Jordan could see Briony and Charlie through the Chowder Hut window. They hovered around a booth at the far end with a group of other seniors. Jordan stood in the doorway for a second, wondering whether she should approach them. Briony soon spotted her and waved her over.

"Hey, what's up?" Jordan said, trying to sound casual as she joined the group.

Everyone was so busy talking over one

another that she thought no one had heard her. But then Briony answered, "Oh, hey Jordan! You made it!"

"Yeah, I didn't have a whole lot else going on. There's not a ton of homework this week." She sounded lame even to herself.

Thankfully, Briony pretended not to notice. "Well, you're just in time," she said cheerfully. "We're plotting our revenge against St. Philomena's."

"What?" Jordan half-laughed. "Revenge?"

"Yes, revenge! They should never have beat us at last year's homecoming, and this time we're going to make sure they don't do it again."

"What are you going to do?" Jordan asked.

Charlie chimed in, "Ah, we're just going to scare 'em a little. Intimidate them so they don't play as well. It's all in good fun."

He smiled at Jordan, and she felt her face flush. How could he be so cute and so cool and nice?

"Good fun? I don't think so," Briony sneered. "After that stunt they pulled yesterday during 'Bridgewater Live,' they're going down. I want to see them crying like babies by the time we're done with them."

Jordan was surprised. She had never seen this tough-girl side of Briony before. But just as she thought she'd misjudged her, Briony thrust her purse into Charlie's hands, saying, "Charlie, can you hold my purse open for a minute? I can't find my lip gloss and hold it at the same time."

He glanced over at Jordan with a sheepish shrug as he held the purse. Jordan looked away, feeling embarrassed for him. Did Briony always push him around like this?

"So, what *is* your plan?" Jordan asked.

"We start at midnight tonight on the roof of St. Philomena's," Briony started. "By tomorrow morning our message will be crystal clear." She looked around at the rest of the group—Kevin, Leslie, Carlos, and Thomas—and they all nodded vigorously along with her. Charlie looked down at his feet.

"You're breaking into the school?" Jordan exclaimed.

"Don't seem so shocked," Briony replied. "You'll be there with us."

"Tonight? I . . . umm . . . I can't do it

tonight." Jordan tried to think of an excuse. The last thing she wanted was to get expelled for pulling some stupid prank. "My grandparents are visiting and staying in my room. I'm supposed to sleep on the couch. My parents will hear me if I try to sneak out."

Briony rolled her eyes. "Fine, then. You can make it up to us tomorrow. Meet us here at the same time in the afternoon, and we'll fill you in on the plan. Hey, you guys wanna order some fries or something?"

"Yeah-uh! And some onion rings. I need a little fuel for tonight's pre-game!" Carlos answered.

Jordan's heart raced as she nodded along. She wanted to just run away, but she wanted to stay, too. She tried to munch on fries and laugh at all the right times. But between her mad crush on Charlie and Briony's strange invitation, it was difficult to act normal.

"Are you going to the game?" Jordan asked Charlie. She realized as soon as she asked it that it was a dumb question—*of course* he would be going to the game. What senior wasn't? She thought she saw Briony smirk, but Charlie pretended not to notice.

"Planning on it. Are you?" he said.

"I guess so. My dad played football for Bridgewater High, so I always try to go."

"Oh yeah? That's cool. My mom was a cheerleader. I wonder if they knew each other," Charlie replied.

"Small world," Jordan replied, and they smiled at each other.

"Alright, it's time to get moving, everyone," Briony commanded. Then she added sarcastically, "Everyone except Jordan, that is. She has to go hang out with her *grandparents.*"

Jordan felt her face get hot as she exited the Chowder Hut. "Have fun," she murmured. "I'll see you tomorrow."

"Oh, wait, Jordan," Briony said, "I almost forgot. None of us have our bikes. We took Charlie's truck to school."

"So?"

"We need to borrow yours. Someone has to be on the lookout on the opposite side of the building, in case someone comes while we're up on the roof."

"But I can't do it tonight."

"You've already made that clear." Briony rolled her eyes. "But if we can use your bike, at least someone else can stay out there to warn us, then bike away without being seen."

"Well, I guess so." Jordan couldn't think of a good reason to say no. She wasn't a good liar as it was. She was surprised they'd believed the story about her grandparents.

Briony stood next to Jordan as she unlocked the bike and handed it over. Briony smiled sweetly. "Thanks. We'll tell you all about it tomorrow!"

On the walk home, the queasy feeling in Jordan's stomach got worse. She went to bed early, but she couldn't sleep. She felt like throwing up.

"It's OK, Jordan," she told herself, taking three big breaths. She tried to make herself better by thinking of Charlie. The way he'd looked at her made her melt inside. He didn't seem nearly as eager to get revenge on St. Philomena's as the others. Maybe tomorrow

21

Jordan would try to hang back and talk to him while the others went through with their next prank.

As she finally drifted off to sleep, a vision of that odd look in Briony's eyes came to Jordan. How determined Briony seemed to get revenge. That night she dreamed about *Cheerleader Slasher*. Except this time, the evil cheerleader was Briony.

When Jordan arrived at school the next day, something was strange. The buzz from the day before seemed to have vanished. Groups of kids huddled near their lockers, whispering. She saw one girl crying in the bathroom.

"Why does everyone look like they're at a funeral? Isn't homecoming week supposed to be full of fun and laughter?" Kit asked grumpily.

Just then, Principal Weston's voice came on the loudspeaker. "Attention students. Please report to the gymnasium immediately for an important announcement."

Kit looked at Jordan quizzically. Jordan shrugged. They made their way to the gymnasium.

Once everyone was settled in the gym, Principal Weston walked slowly up to a podium with a microphone.

"Students and teachers," Principal Weston began. "I regret to inform you that a tragedy has befallen us. Carlos Perez fell off the roof of St. Philomena's last night. He is currently hospitalized and in a comatose state."

Jordan couldn't believe it. Carlos in a coma? He had been ordering onion rings and laughing with everyone just the night before at the Chowder Hut. Something had gone terribly wrong with Briony's prank.

"Our thoughts are with Carlos and his family as we maintain hope that he recovers quickly and to full capacity. This weekend's game will go on as planned." The principal cleared his throat and raised his voice. "We have reason to believe that Carlos was taking part in a prank related to the upcoming football game. I want to impress upon all of you that dangerous antics of this sort will not be tolerated at Bridgewater High."

Jordan scanned the room, but she couldn't find Charlie, Briony, or the others.

"Furthermore, we suspect that Carlos was not alone last night. The police received an anonymous call reporting the accident shortly after 12:30 A.M. We expect whoever made that call to come forward immediately. There was also a red bicycle with a blue basket left on the lawn of the school. If any of you know someone who rides such a bicycle, please report to my office today."

Kit looked at her, wide-eyed. "Your bike?" she mouthed.

But Jordan couldn't answer. Carlos fell from the roof? How did it happen?

The principal dismissed the students. Somehow, Jordan made her way back to class with the rest of the shocked students.

"What was he doing on the roof in the first place?" she heard one guy say to another. "It doesn't make any sense."

"Do you think he jumped on purpose?" said the other.

As the day went on, students seemed to lighten up. Someone passed a gigantic get-well card around the school and everyone signed it. But Jordan couldn't shake the bad feeling in her gut. Was Carlos going to live? What had happened that night? What if someone found out the bike left behind was hers and blamed her? She couldn't believe she would have to wait until after school to find out what happened.

Jordan dreaded another encounter with Briony, but she needed to learn more about the previous night's accident. When she finally got to the Chowder Hut, she found the same group—minus Carlos—sitting in the same corner booth.

"I thought I was the only one not wearing flannels or a negligee," Jordan said, trying out an awkward joke about pajama day as she sat down next to Charlie.

"Only freshmen and losers wear pajamas to school," Briony replied coldly. "Besides, we have more important things to worry about, like how to toilet paper Judd Powell's house tonight without getting caught." Judd Powell was St. Philomena's star quarterback.

"You mean you want to go through with another prank?" Jordan asked. "I thought, after what happened to Carlos—"

Briony cut her off. "*Of course* we're going through with it! What happened to Carlos was an accident, pure and simple! He's going to come out of this and be super mad if we don't finish the job!"

Jordan looked at the rest of the group. Everyone seemed to nod in agreement. Charlie looked at her with a half-smile on his face, as if he didn't know what to think.

"What *did* happen to Carlos?" Jordan whispered.

The table was quiet for a moment. Finally, Leslie spoke. "It was so weird. We'd broken into the school and made it up to the roof where we were going to hang our sign. Bri and I went to one side of the roof. Carlos was on the other side, about ten feet away from us. Kev and Thomas were untangling the ropes so we could use them to tie up the sign."

"I was driving the getaway car," said Charlie.

"What about my bike? Who was on lookout duty?"

"Oh, we scratched that plan," Briony said, as if it made perfect sense. "Once we got there, we realized we didn't need a lookout after all."

How convenient, Jordan thought. "So you just left it there?"

"Well, we kinda forgot about the stupid bike once our friend got hurt!" Briony said sharply. Jordan felt like a huge jerk.

Leslie continued, "Yeah, so we painted this huge sheet in big black letters, *We will cut your Yellowthroats.*"

Jordan understood the reference—the Yellowthroat was St. Philomena's school mascot, named after a common New England bird—but that didn't make the image any less gruesome.

"So," Leslie went on, "Carlos was alone on that side of the roof, holding the other side of the banner. Then all the sudden I heard this gasp, and then Carlos was screaming, 'No no no no!' Then we felt this tug at the other end of the banner. By the time I looked up, he had already fallen off."

Jordan shivered. Leslie's eyes were glistening and huge as she looked right at Jordan. "The way he screamed—it was as if he were screaming *at* someone. And then I heard this wailing sound. At first I thought it was him, but it sounded like a girl crying."

"What could it have been?" Jordan asked.

"I have no idea, but it sounded like someone else was there!" Leslie was shivering.

"Will you guys cut it out? You're getting all creeped out over nothing," Kevin said.

Jordan wasn't so sure, but she decided not to argue. "So, did you guys take him to the hospital then?"

"Well, not exactly . . ." Charlie said. "I wanted to take him, but Briony thought it was better not to move him."

"We called the police from a pay phone, then parked where they couldn't see us to make sure they came to get him," Briony explained.

"You just *left* him there?" Jordan couldn't believe it.

"We were freaking out! We didn't know what to do. Plus, what good would it do if we got caught?" Briony sounded defensive.

"We should have stayed," Charlie said quietly.

"There's nothing we can do about it now. Now we have to figure out how to beat Powell without Carlos. I bet this was all a trap by those St. Philomena's lowlifes—to ruin one of our best players. We can't let them get away with it!" Briony declared.

"Well, I don't care what happened," Leslie retorted. "That was the weirdest sound I've ever heard. I'm not going anywhere tonight."

"Suit yourself, wuss. At least there are two big girls around here." Briony glanced at Jordan. Leslie just rolled her eyes and began to gather her bag and jacket. "Whatever you say." Jordan was tempted to get up and follow Leslie right out the door. She could feel Briony's eyes on her, almost daring her to do so. Still, doing more pranks seemed like a bad idea.

Jordan looked straight at Briony and said, "I think you should forget about this. These stunts are dangerous. I'm sure you don't want anyone else getting hurt."

"No way are we backing down, but you can if you want. Of course, all it takes is a phone call to Principal Weston mentioning a certain red bicycle, and you're just as guilty as the rest of us." Briony smiled her sugar-sweet smile.

Jordan felt rage like a clenched fist in her stomach. *So that's why Briony invited me in the first place,* she thought. *So they'd have someone to blame if they got caught. I'll show her I'm not afraid of pranks or her.*

Plus, Jordan reasoned, t*hat means more time with Charlie.*

Jordan smiled just as sweetly back at Briony when she said, "So, what's the plan tonight?"

Briony actually squealed with excitement.

Briony laid out the plan: "We'll make a stop at Kevin's dad's vet clinic to pick up the supplies. Then we'll head to Judd's."

Briony explained that Judd lived about a quarter mile from the southern point of the harbor at the end of a cul-de-sac. Woods surrounded his house. They would park at the harbor, then snake through the trees to the front of the house.

Briony decided that she would ride with Charlie while Kevin, Thomas, and Jordan crammed into Kevin's messy car. Jordan wasn't surprised that Briony had engineered even the carpooling so that she could have Charlie to herself.

That night Kevin and Thomas picked Jordan up at her house. When she got in the car, the guys immediately turned on the classic rock station at full volume and started screaming along to "Born to Run." They decided to pull through the Wendy's drive-through for Frosties before meeting Briony and Charlie at the clinic. For the first time that night, Jordan was having fun. She even forgot about the prank for a little while. When they finally arrived at the vet clinic, Briony was fuming.

"Where were you guys?" Briony demanded as the three of them ambled out of Kevin's car, each sucking on their straws. "We've been waiting here for like ten minutes!"

"Hey, a man's gotta eat," Kevin replied.

"What's *her* excuse?" Briony gestured toward Jordan. Jordan was really starting to get annoyed with this side of Briony.

"A girl's gotta eat," Jordan replied, doing her best impersonation of Kevin. The three boys snickered.

Briony huffed, "Let's just get going already!"

Charlie laughed a little from behind Briony's back and then turned to Jordan, saying, "You know, I asked my mom if she knew your dad. I guess he was a couple classes older than her, but she knew who he was."

"Oh really? That's so cool!" Jordan was flattered that Charlie had remembered their conversation.

"Yeah, small world. Just like you said." Charlie smiled slightly.

Kevin led everyone around to the back entrance where the vet's assistants took the dogs out for walks. He opened the double lock and punched a code into the keypad. The door clicked open.

"Now, we've got to be super quiet while we're in here," Kevin whispered. "We don't want all the animals to start howling."

He led them into a back room. A bunch of medical supplies in white boxes sat stacked on metal shelves. "Grab a few of those garbage bags, and let's start filling 'em up," he instructed.

Jordan started for the industrial toilet paper rolls. "How much do we need?"

"About five times that amount!" Kevin laughed. "If we run out of toilet paper, start grabbing paper towels."

"Won't your dad get mad if we take all this stuff?" Jordan asked.

Kevin shook his head. "He's kind of spacey. I worked here over the summer. It was a lame job, so I just started taking supplies. One time I took thirty rolls of toilet paper. We t.p.'d Lawrence Adams's house—covered the whole yard. They're still probably pulling toilet paper out of trees. Anyway, my dad never said a thing, just ordered more stuff."

"Hey, what's in there?" Briony asked. She has standing in front of a large metal door.

"Oh, that's the freezer," Kevin explained. "They keep some of the meds in there. If any animals die, they go in there too until animal services can come out to pick 'em up."

"Are there dead dogs and cats in there right now?" Jordan asked.

"Maybe. Let's look," Kevin replied.

"*Ewwww!*" Briony squealed, though she sounded more delighted than grossed out.

They followed Kevin into the freezer as he flipped on the light. He motioned to a zipped white bag on the floor. "That looks about sixty-some pounds. Probably a small retriever or something."

"Can we see it?" Thomas asked.

"I guess so." Kevin shrugged and bent down to unzip the bag. Jordan backed away but stayed in the freezer. She couldn't decide if she was more grossed out or curious.

They stood for a moment studying the animal. It was stiff and pale yellow. It almost didn't even look like a real dog.

Briony squealed again. "Let's take it!" she exclaimed. "We can hang it from Judd's tree!"

"Oh man, that's just *wrong*!" said Kevin.

"Exactly what I was thinking," said Jordan. "It was someone's pet!"

"Come on! It will totally freak him out!" Briony argued.

"It *would* be kind of perfect—totally creepy," Thomas agreed.

"Stealing toilet paper is a little different from stealing a dog," Kevin mumbled weakly. Charlie was just silent.

"What?" Briony demanded. "Don't wimp out on us, Kevin."

Don't do it! Jordan wanted to shout. Before she could, Kevin replied, "Fine, but you guys have to carry it. It's gonna be *heavy.*"

***

Charlie and Thomas managed to hoist the dead, frozen dog and carry it out of the clinic while Kevin locked the door behind them.

"Are you sure your dad's not going to notice a missing dead dog?" Jordan asked him in one last, lame attempt to abort the mission.

"Nah, and he wouldn't blame me even if he did notice," Kevin said.

They loaded the dog and supplies into Kevin's trunk and started toward the harbor parking lot. Each time they braked, the dog thudded against the back seat.

This is sick, Jordan thought. *I should go home.* But there was no way Briony would pause the plans to wait for Kevin to bring her home. She'd have to stick it out.

When the group finally parked, they had to maneuver the dog out of the car again. Charlie and Thomas kept complaining about how heavy it was. Finally Kevin agreed to help them carry it. The five of them made their way through the trees in the dark. At one point, Thomas stumbled and they almost dropped the animal.

"Careful!" Briony snapped.

Jordan couldn't believe she had ever thought this girl was perfect and nice.

There's no way Charlie likes her, Jordan thought.

A few orange lights were strung along the shrubs in Judd's yard, early Halloween decorations. The group set the dog on the ground and began spreading the toilet paper over the trees. Jordan tried to work quickly, nervous that Judd's parents would wake up and catch them. The others were snickering and giggling.

"*Shhhh*, you guys!" Jordan pleaded.

Once they had gone through all the toilet paper, Briony waved them over. "You guys! Let's tie a noose around the dog. We can hang it from a tree. It'll totally freak Judd out."

"Does anyone know how?" Kevin asked.

"I think I can figure it out," Charlie said.

Briony pulled out a rope from her bag, left over from hanging the sign at St. Philomena's. Charlie worked quickly while Kevin removed the dog from the bag. Charlie went to test the rope by looping it around the dog's neck.

"That's not how you do it! We have to hang it from a branch first, then lift the dog up to it. Otherwise it'll get all mangled before we can tighten the noose," whispered Thomas.

Charlie whispered back, "Alright, but you do it."

"Just give me the rope." Thomas sounded impatient.

Thomas spotted a thick branch about seven feet up on a nearby oak. He found a lawn chair near the house, carried it over, and climbed up on it. When he was finished securing the rope to the branch, he instructed, "Alright, two of us will lift the dog into the noose, and the other one will pull it tight around the neck. Ready? Charlie, you tighten it."

But Charlie just looked at the dead dog. "No way! This is nasty. Kevin, you do it."

"Come on, you guys, it's easy. See?" Thomas put his own head through the noose and started to grin. "And then you just yank it." He pulled on the long end of the rope to demonstrate. He pretended to gag. "Spooky, right? I think I'll make this my Halloween costume next year."

"Man, let's just get this over with—" Kevin started to hoist the dog.

Then he stopped. Everyone froze. Thomas was gasping and gulping for air.

Horrified, Jordan could see Thomas's feet kicking frantically in the air. The chair had been knocked aside! Thomas clawed desperately at the rope around his neck.

"Oh my god!" Jordan cried.

A slow gurgling sound started coming from Thomas's throat. Briony shrieked, then crumpled to the ground and started bawling uncontrollably.

Charlie leapt in the air, trying to reach Thomas, but Thomas was too high up. Meanwhile, Kevin tried to set the chair up under Thomas, but Thomas gave a powerful kick that sent him flying backwards.

"We have to get him down now! He's choking!" Charlie shouted again. "Kev, get up!"

Kevin looked dazed. "He's powerful, man."

Jordan rushed to Charlie's side. The moon had vanished. She could barely make out Thomas's legs as they scissor-kicked in the air. She tried to grab one leg to steady him while Charlie set up the chair and stood on it. He reached up and tried to loosen the rope around

Thomas's neck. Then Thomas kicked hard and knocked Jordan aside.

"Come on, man! Just let me untie this!" Charlie shouted. But it was as if Thomas was struggling against them, resisting their help.

Then, all of a sudden, Thomas's body went completely limp. Charlie quickly loosened the rope and pulled him to the ground.

"He's not breathing!" Charlie screamed.

Jordan could hear a low wailing sound echoing behind her in the dark.

"Briony, stop crying and call an ambulance!" Charlie shouted. "I'm going to try CPR."

"That wasn't me!" Briony yelled out. Jordan was surprised to realize Briony wasn't behind her after all. For a split second she wondered where the wailing had been coming from. But there was no time to think about anything but getting Thomas to breathe again.

Briony got on her phone and called 911. Charlie kept breathing into Thomas's mouth.

But it was no use. By the time the ambulance came, Jordan knew Thomas had died. She found herself surrounded by several police officers, demanding answers she didn't even know how to deliver. Judd Powell and his parents, who had been awakened by the noise, came out of the house. For a minute they just stood there, frozen, taking in the scene: toilet paper everywhere, a frozen dog, and a lifeless teenage boy sprawled on the ground.

Mr. and Mrs. Powell stood on their doorstep, shocked at the sight. Judd's face went white, and his lips seemed to disappear for a minute. Then he just lost it.

"What the hell were you thinking?" he screamed at the Bridgewater crew. "This is sick! All of you are sick!"

Charlie, his face wet with tears and sweat, could do little more than shake his head. Kevin had gone grey-faced and silent. But Briony lashed out at Judd.

"This is all *your* fault, with your *cheating* team and that crazy trap you set on the roof!" she screamed.

A few officers pulled Jordan aside and wrapped a blanket around her shoulders. She was in shock. How could this have happened? Two days ago she'd never even spoken to these people. Now one of them was *dead*, and it was partly her fault.

Jordan took a deep breath and told the police everything she could remember, including the part about her bicycle in the rooftop prank.

Somehow Jordan got through the police questioning. The second round of questioning began when a squad car dropped her off at two in the morning.

"How could this have happened? Breaking into a veterinary clinic? Stealing a dead dog? Trespassing?" Jordan's dad hadn't even mentioned the worst detail of all—Thomas's death.

Jordan tried to stay clam. She knew her dad was upset, but there was no use in trying to explain the unexplainable. She couldn't keep her tears from running. Her mother came to her side to comfort her.

"I don't know who this new crowd is that you're hanging around with. There was a group like that when I was at Bridgewater. They were always pulling pranks. But those tricks can have real consequences. If you're not careful, you'll end up just like . . . like . . ." her father trailed off.

"Like who?" Jordan asked through her sniffles. But her father was already walking away. In the early morning light, she could detect deep lines of worry and sadness on his face.

"Who, Dad?" she tried again.

"Nobody!" her father snapped. The look on his face had gone from sad to angry. Jordan had never seen him look like this, and it scared her. He shook his head and quickly left the room.

Inconsolable, Jordan cried herself to sleep on the couch, images of Thomas's twitching form and the low wailing sound that had accompanied his last breaths haunting her dreams.

9

I t felt weird for Jordan to wake up and go to
school the next day as if everything were
normal. At first, the police had threatened that
she and the other kids could be suspended
or even expelled. But it soon became clear
that since the pranks hadn't occurred on
Bridgewater High property, the only legal
action against them would come from St.
Philomena's or Judd Powell's parents. Jordan
and the others would have to wait to find
out if anyone was pressing charges. In the

meantime, Jordan's parents had forced her to go to school.

When she arrived, her hair unwashed and face still puffy, her nightmare only worsened. What looked like half the school was gathered around the edge of the football field to the right of the main building. Teachers and administrators stood around, trying to urge them inside the building. A familiar sense of dread began to build in Jordan. She made her way slowly toward the crowd.

In the center of the field lay a pickup truck, flipped over and smashed in several places. An ambulance was parked next to the bashed vehicle, and two paramedics were pulling out a stretcher. The truck must have been driven all over the field, as the turf was completely ripped up.

"What the . . ." Jordan started. Then she saw him, the driver, wedged under the vehicle. *Dead.* He wore a St. Philomena's letter jacket. It had been another prank. Another prank gone wrong.

"Noooooooooo!" Jordan screamed. "Nooooo!" She couldn't stop herself. She was still screaming when Charlie and Kit appeared, rushing from the crowd.

They took her inside the building and sat down with her on a bench near the cafeteria. Charlie bought her a Sprite from the vending machines. She sipped it slowly, trying to clam her anxiety.

"Are you OK?" Kit finally asked.

"I guess I'm just so shaken up by everything that's happened," Jordan replied. She felt totally exhausted.

"I know how you feel," Charlie finally answered. Then, lowering his voice, he said, "I couldn't stop him last night. No matter what I did. I couldn't get a hold of him. I couldn't save him."

"And that horrible wailing. I can't get it out of my mind," Jordan added.

"What are you talking about?" Kit demanded.

"It's a long story. I'll have to fill you in after creative writing class," Jordan told Kit, glancing at the clock. But she was a little worried about getting her best friend involved in this mess.

"OK, you'd better," Kit replied.

"I'll catch up with you later," Charlie said with a sad smile. *He looks how I feel*, Jordan thought, studying the deep circles underneath his eyes.

B y the time Kit and Jordan got to class, everyone knew about what had happened that morning on the football field. One of Judd's teammates had decided to send a little message of his own. He drove his truck onto the field and started to shred the grass. He hoped school officials would move the game to St. Philomena's, where students would be prepared to bomb the visitors' section with water balloons and eggs.

But something had gone wrong. Though police investigators could find nothing defective within the vehicle, they determined that it had somehow spun out and flipped. The driver's neck snapped—he died instantly, alone. He was Bridgewater's second teen death in less than six hours.

Jordan was glad to be in creative writing class. If anyone could make her feel better, it was Mr. Brown.

"Alright, everyone," Mr. Brown began, "I know a lot has happened over the past few days, and creative writing might be the last thing on your mind. But sometimes when you're going through a difficult time, it can help to put your feelings down on paper."

"I'm going to ask that you use the first twenty minutes of our class time today to write freely about whatever you're thinking about. Don't worry about grammar or spelling or anyone reading what you write. Just write your emotions down. And Ms. Windsor, please refrain from poking Brian's head with that pencil. I'm sure he doesn't appreciate it."

Jordan managed to smile a little at Mr. Brown's familiar way of calling out the students. She felt her phone vibrate. She peeked at the screen inside her bag. Kit had sent her a text from across the room: *It's a touchy-feely day in Mr. Rogers' neighborhood.*

Jordan smiled a little in spite of herself. Even in the worst of situations, Kit somehow managed to crack jokes.

Jordan began to write down everything that had happened over the past few days. She started with Monday in the gym—"Bridgewater Live." The next day Carlos had fallen from the rooftop, and Leslie had heard that weird crying sound. Leslie's description of the crying had sounded almost exactly like what she had heard at Judd Powell's. But how could that possibly be? And why would she and Leslie hear the same thing in two completely different places? Then, just this morning, the St. Philomena's student had died trying to tear up the football field. Three accidents and two deaths in less than four days. It didn't even feel real.

Jordan's concentration was broken by the sound of someone crying out in pain. She scanned the room and saw that Kelsey Windsor was holding a palm up to one eye.

"Kelsey, what happened? Are you OK?" Mr. Brown rushed to her side.

"My eye!" she yelped, pulling her hand away just long enough for Jordan to glimpse blood pouring from Kelsey's face onto her desk. Kelsey jumped up and began spastically wiping the blood from her hands onto the back of Brian McGuire's blue button-down.

"You did this!" she screamed. "It's your fault!"

Suddenly, Jordan heard a familiar low wail coming from behind her. She didn't turn around because she knew there would be nothing to see. *No!* she thought. *Stop it! This has to stop now!*

"I didn't mean to . . ." Brian looked pale and stricken. He couldn't seem to get a complete sentence out. "She kept poking me. I was just trying to take the pencil away and . . ."

"Why don't you go get yourself cleaned up?" Mr. Brown said to Brian. He pulled Kelsey away from Brian and led her out the classroom door. Her screams of pain trailed back into the classroom from the hall.

Brian looked blank. The rest of the class stared at him in disbelief.

Finally Kit said, "What the hell happened, Brian?"

He shook his head. "I don't know. I don't know how that could have happened. I think I'm going to be sick." Brian made a move for the door, cupping his hands over his mouth.

Jordan had heard enough. There were way too many accidents for it all to be just a coincidence. Something was going on, and she had to figure out what it was. She jumped up from her desk, crossed the room, and grabbed Kit by the wrist.

"We've got to get out of here!" she hissed, quiet enough that the other students wouldn't hear her. For once in her life, Kit actually did what she was told.

Once they were alone in the hallway, Jordan turned to Kit.

"Look," she said, "Something strange is going on here. I don't know what it is, but this isn't normal. But I need you to tell me if I'm crazy, OK?"

Kit hesitated. For a second, Jordan thought Kit might just laugh at her, but instead Kit said, "OK, tell me what's going on."

Jordan took a deep breath and told Kit everything that had happened, in detail. She even told her about the weird sounds she'd been hearing.

"Oh my god! That's too creepy! I think you're right. Something way weird is going on. What do you think is causing all of this?" Kit asked.

"I'm not totally sure," Jordan replied. "My dad said something last night. Something about kids doing pranks when he was at Bridgewater and it turning out badly. He got really upset. Do you know what he's talking *about*?"

Kit shook her head. "No idea."

"I'm going to the library."

"You're gonna skip? What for? You'll miss chemistry. We have a test . . ."

"I have to see if I can find any clues to make sense of this crazy mess. I need to try something. You go ahead to class."

"OK," Kit said tentatively. "Good luck. You know where to find me." She waved her phone in the air as they parted ways.

At Bridgewater Public Library, Jordan began her search. She looked up every archived article she could find about Bridgewater in the 1970s, when her dad was in high school. She read speeches from the town mayor, legal documents, and obituaries. Hours passed, and she had nothing.

She was about to give up when she spotted a brief one-paragraph piece in a more recent edition of the *Bridgewater Gazette*.

> *Hydroponic Greenhouse Produce Grown Locally*
>
> *Bridgewater native Devon Morton recently began selling hydroponic produce from a greenhouse he constructed himself several years ago in the neighboring town of Clintsville. Morton downplays interest in organic food or the environment, stating that this endeavor is "just a way to make an earning while living alone out here." Morton settled in his Clintsville property after graduating from Bridgewater High in 1975. When asked what prompted the move, Morton simply replied, "bad memories." In addition to hydroponic farming, Morton sells handcrafted*

miniature figurines and other goods. To place a produce delivery order, visit www .mortonproduce.com.

Jordan's reread the last lines a few times. 1975? '*Bad memories*'? She quickly e-mailed the article to herself. *It could be nothing*, Jordan thought. *But if Dad won't talk to me, maybe this guy will have something to say.*

She set about trying to find more information online, but there was no use. Frustrated, she decided to ask the librarian if she could browse through old yearbooks.

"Ms. Kindal?" Jordan said, approaching the reference desk. "May I look through some old Bridgewater High yearbooks?"

"Oh dear, why in the world would you want to look through those old things?" Ms. Kindal replied with a kind smile.

"Well, I just want to see one, actually, from 1975. We're doing a project in my—"

"We don't have *that* year," Ms. Kindal interrupted her abruptly, her smile gone and her voice much harsher now. Jordan leaned back, surprised.

"Oh, well, I just thought, you know, since that was the year my uncle graduated . . ." Jordan was trying to think fast.

"Your uncle?" Ms. Kindal peered at her.

"Yeah, Mr. Morton. Devon Morton." Jordan gulped.

Ms. Kindal's voice became quiet, and she smiled sweetly at Jordan again. "I'm sorry. We don't have what you're looking for here."

Jordan practically ran away from creepy Ms. Kindal. It was all getting way too weird.

Jordan pushed through the hallway at Bridgewater High, making her way to the southeast stairwell. She passed Kevin at his locker.

"Hey, Kev. How're you feeling?" she asked, touching his shoulder lightly.

He flinched, and she quickly pulled her hand back. "Sorry, I just wanted to say hi."

"Hey," he said, not looking at her. "You getting pumped for the game?"

"The game?" Jordan asked, confused.

"Jordan, you're so clueless sometimes," he said, starting to laugh. "The homecoming game? This Friday?"

Why was he acting so weird? Jordan wondered.

"But I thought it was canceled."

"Why would it be canceled?" Kevin finally looked at her. His eyes looked glazed.

"Kevin? Is everything all right?"

"Sure. It's going to be a blast. Talk to Briony. We're all gonna meet up beforehand. I gotta run. We've got an extra-long practice today." With that, Kevin swung his gym bag around his shoulder and started off down the hallway.

Jordan stood there speechless for a second. Then she felt a tug at her sweater that made her jump.

"Chill out, it's just me," Kit said flatly. "Any luck at the library?"

"I found this one article that mentioned something about Bridgewater High in 1975. Like something bad had happened. But then I couldn't find anything else online. I tried to check out something old from that time, like a yearbook or something, but that crazy old Ms. Kindal wouldn't let me see any."

"Hmm, that's weird. Well, you know my dad keeps everything. Maybe he's got something buried in the garage. Should we skip last period and check it out?" Kit asked.

Jordan nodded. "Yes, but let's find Charlie first."

Kit raised her eyebrows and smiled.

Jordan blushed a little. "It's not that," she explained. "I just think he'd want to know about this. Maybe he can help."

Kit looped an arm through Jordan's as they combed the hallways, searching for Charlie. They peered into different classrooms and study hall, too. They passed by two seniors making out under the stairwell.

How can everyone just carry on like nothing is wrong? Jordan wondered. And why wasn't school canceled, either?

"Hey, Kevin just invited me to go to the football game with him and Briony on Friday night," Jordan told Kit.

"So?" Kit replied.

"So . . . isn't the game canceled?"

"Apparently not. While you were buried in the library today, Principal Weston made another announcement. They're just hosting the game at St. Philomena's instead. Everyone cheered. It was the stupidest thing I'd ever heard."

"Seriously!? I thought Kevin was in shock from last night! Doesn't anyone feel the need to mourn the deaths of two students? What reason could they possibly have for not canceling the game?"

"Principal Weston just said that he had talked with St. Philomena's principal. They both decided that the schools ought to come together, blah blah blah. Honestly, it sounded to me like they were afraid something worse would happen if the game were canceled," Kit explained.

Suddenly, Jordan spotted Charlie heading toward the back exit that led to the parking lot.

"Charlie, wait!" Jordan hollered. She jogged to catch up with him. "Where are you going?"

"I just got a call from Carlos's parents. They're at the hospital. Carlos just woke up, and he's asking for me. I have to go see him."

"Can I go with you?" Jordan asked breathlessly.

"OK, but, uh, maybe just you?" He looked at Kit. "He's been in a coma, you know. I don't want to freak him out with a ton of visitors."

"It's cool," Kit said. "You guys do your thing. I'll find the yearbooks, and you can come by after the hospital to check 'em out."

"Thanks, Kit," Jordan said, following Charlie to his car.

On the way to the hospital, Jordan told Charlie all about what happened in creative writing with Kelsey Windsor's eye.

"Sounds worse than what happened in PE this afternoon," he said.

"What are you talking about?"

"Chen Miller was trying to mess with the new kid. The kid's kinda little, not much taller than you." Charlie gave Jordan a sideways half-smile, and she felt her heart flip-flop. "Anyway, Chen was being a bully, chasing the poor guy around the gym during dodgeball. At one point the kid darted in the other direction to avoid getting hit. Chen tried to follow him, but he's too clumsy. He stumbled a few times and took a faceplant right into that metal container where they keep all the balls. Totally knocked him out."

"Wow." Jordan said.

"Yeah, well, the really weird thing is . . . I heard that wailing cry again when he fell. It was the same thing I heard when Thomas was . . . killed. All these deaths . . . I'm starting to think something really bad is happening."

"I was just telling Kit! It's like we're cursed or something!" Jordan exclaimed. She explained what she'd learned in the library.

"My mom would've been in school back in '75 too. But she doesn't talk much about her high school days—I know she was a cheerleader, and that's about it. I hope Kit finds something in the yearbooks. Maybe Carlos can give us more answers, too," Charlie said. "So, Kit—is she like your best friend or something?"

"Yeah, since we were pretty little. She's awesome. I mean, it takes a little while for her to let down her guard. But once you're in, she's a great friend."

"That's really cool." Charlie seemed to be paying a lot of attention to what she was saying. "Sometimes I wish my friends were more like that."

"What do you mean?" Jordan couldn't believe she and Charlie were having this conversation.

"Well, like Briony, for example. She thinks everybody likes her or wants to be her or something, but sometimes she treats people like crap. Like, that whole thing with your bike was super lame." Charlie turned toward her. "I didn't have anything to do with that, you know."

"I didn't think you did. But thanks," Jordan replied.

They pulled up to the hospital and parked in the visitors' section. Jordan started to get out, but Charlie came around and opened the door for her. *This is almost feeling datelike*, she thought, *except for the whole visiting-a-friend-in-the-hospital-after-a-series-of-random-accidents.* Not quite the same as a movie and dinner. Still, she smiled a little.

At the front desk Charlie talked to a receptionist with bright pink lipstick. "We're here to see Carlos Perez."

"Sure, sweetheart. He's sure had a lot of visitors! You can head down to room 303."

"I wonder who's visited so far," Jordan said to Charlie as she followed him down the hall.

"Probably family—Carlos has a really big family."

But as they were about to enter the door to Carlos's room, they came face-to-face with Briony coming out. She looked tired, and her hair was messy. *Probably for the first time in her life*, Jordan thought.

"Hey, what's going on?" said Charlie, surprised.

Briony fixed her eyes on Jordan, then narrowed them at Charlie. "I came to visit our good friend in the hospital, obviously," she said. She glared at Jordan.

"Us too. How is he?" Charlie asked.

"He seems to be doing OK. I told him everything that's been going on around school, and he's pissed. He definitely doesn't want that game to take place on St. Philomena's field."

"There's nothing we can do about it. Our field is torn up. Both principals decided to move it to St. P's. It's a done deal," Charlie explained.

"St. P's? What are they, like, your friends now or something? You going to transfer there?"

"Briony, what are you talking about?" Charlie looked bewildered. He put a hand on her shoulder. "Maybe you should go home and get some sleep. This week has been hard on all of us."

Briony shrugged him off. "*Sleep?* The last thing I need is sleep at a time like this. Look, I expect you to show up tomorrow night to help us. Five o'clock." She looked at Charlie intensely, then at Jordan. "You, too. Be there."

With that, Briony sauntered off.

"What was that all about? Be where?" said

Charlie. "I swear that girl is crazy sometimes."

Jordan was surprised that Charlie didn't seem to think Briony was being more extreme than usual.

Her expression must have shown what she was thinking.

"What?" Charlie asked her.

"Didn't you think she was behaving strangely? Like, stranger than usual?"

"I guess so," he said, frowning. "Ready to see Carlos?"

Carlos was sitting up in bed, reading a magazine. He smiled when he saw Charlie.

"Hey, man! Lookin' good." Charlie put one hand up for a high five. He affectionately tapped Carlos's shoulder with the other. Jordan stayed a few feet behind them. She felt a little uncomfortable all of a sudden.

"Hey!" He smiled again and nodded in Jordan's direction. She waved and gave him a little smile.

"So you're awake. How long were you out?" Charlie said.

"Since Monday night, man, when this all went down. I guess the fall knocked me unconscious. I went under. Just woke up a few hours ago."

"Where are your folks?"

"Oh, they haven't left this room for days. When Briony got here, they skipped out to grab a bite in the cafeteria. I hope they bring me some more Jell-O."

The three of them chuckled. Carlos continued, "Speaking of Briony, she was acting pretty weird. She said there's been more accidents or something since my fall. She wouldn't really get into the details. Just kept talking about kicking St. Philomena's butt."

Charlie took a deep breath. Jordan thought she saw his eyes well up with tears. "It's been a rough week, but we don't have to get into all that right now. You should probably relax so you can get outta this place, right?" Charlie tried to smile.

"I guess so." Carlos frowned. "You sure there's nothing I should know about?"

"Nah, man."

Jordan was about to speak up when the door opened and Carlos's parents walked in, arms loaded with snacks and beverages.

"Hey, Mr. and Mrs. Perez." Charlie turned to greet them. He made a move to help them unload their stuff, and they started asking him questions about school and the soccer season. Jordan saw her opportunity and made her way to Carlos's bed.

"Carlos, was there anything that you remember about that night on the roof?" He looked at her quizzically. "Look," Jordan continued, "I think something is wrong. Really, really wrong. If there was anything weird that you remember from your fall, or any strange sounds . . . please tell me."

His eyes darkened. "I can't remember much. It was dark, and it happened so fast. But I still can't figure out how I could have fallen. I was standing, practically crouching a few feet from the ledge. Just waiting for the girls to get ready so we could hang the stupid banner. Then all of a sudden I was being pulled forward."

"Pulled?"

"Yeah, I can't explain it. It was like I had no control against this . . . force."

"A force? What do you—"

"How's my sweetie?" Carlos's mother had

approached the bed and now kissed her son's forehead. "Are you tired? Do you need to go back to sleep?"

Carlos laughed. "Mom, I've been sleeping for three days!"

"We're gonna take off," Charlie said. He came up to high five Carlos again. "Take it easy, man. I'll come back over the weekend."

Back in the car, Charlie seemed a little more at ease.

"You didn't want to tell him about Thomas?" Jordan asked gently.

He shook his head. "He just came out of some serious trauma. I thought it'd be better to let him relax with his family before getting him involved in this whole mess."

"Makes sense," Jordan said.

Charlie turned and gave her another one of his heart-melting smiles. "You're a cool girl."

Jordan blushed. "Thanks."

"Before all this went down, I was thinking about . . ." Charlie stammered. "I was going to ask you to that dance . . ."

Why is the timing always so perfectly off in my life? Jordan thought. She didn't know what to say, so she just started yammering. "Yeah, it's kind of hard to imagine dancing in the midst of all this craziness, I guess."

"Yeah, I guess," Charlie agreed.

They were both quiet for a moment. Jordan broke the awkward silence and told him what Carlos had told her about being *forced* into his fall from the roof.

"Hmm . . ." Charlie thought for a minute. "Remember how I couldn't get Thomas to be still long enough to untie that rope?"

Jordan nodded.

Charlie continued, "It was like there was this powerful resistance. It took everything in my power not to go flying, like Kevin did when Thomas kicked him."

"I hope we find something in the yearbooks," Jordan said.

"Me, too," Charlie said. "For all of our sakes."

When they got to Kit's, they found her in the garage with a bandanna tied around her head and dust covering each palm. There were old boxes all around her. She pulled books out one by one.

"Looks like you've been busy," Jordan said. She and Charlie started pulling books out of boxes too.

"Is this what you want?" Charlie asked. He was holding up a yearbook from 1973.

Jordan shook her head. "Are there more in there?"

He lifted a few more books out and set them aside. Then Jordan saw it: *Bridgewater High Yearbook 1975*. The three of them sat down on the garage floor and began thumbing through the pages. There were photos of each student by year, along with quotes they had picked. They spotted Charlie's mom, looking young and beautiful. Page after page contained students in theater costumes or basketball jerseys, or just studying.

"Look at those dresses!" Kit exclaimed, laughing at the long chiffon gowns with puffed sleeves from that year's prom. Jordan felt a twinge of regret that she wouldn't get to go to the dance with Charlie after all.

They turned to a page that looked somehow different from the rest. It took a few seconds for Jordan to realize why. Then it came to her. "All the students are crying," she said slowly. "Yeah, that's weird." Charlie squinted at the photograph. "Where are they?"

"It looks like some kind of memorial or something," Kit said. "Do you see the candles everyone is holding? And everyone is wearing black."

They turned to another page with the words "Gilbert Sullivan 1958–1975" at the top.

"He died," Charlie said quietly.

There was a picture of Gilbert at the top, and they had printed handwritten letters to him below it.

> *Dear Gilbert,*
> *Wonderful son, we will love you and think of you always. You are in a better place. Love, your adoring Mom and Dad*

> *Gibby,*
> *I won't forget you. You'll always be my best friend.*
> *Dev*

"Devon Morton," Jordan said quietly.

"Huh?" Charlie asked. Jordan quickly explained the article that she'd found.

"Hey, look. Here's another one! A girl this time." Kit opened to a page that read "Elizabeth Barton, 1958–1975." There was a photo of a pretty girl with a big, toothy smile and long shiny hair. *She looks like Briony*, Jordan thought.

They turned more pages to see the smiling faces of Peter Jacobsen and Theodore Moran. Then there was Chelsea Knight, 1960–1975. Chelsea wore a lavender turtleneck. Her hair was parted down the middle and braided. She wasn't smiling.

"She looks shy," Kit remarked.

"She's younger than the others. Just fifteen," said Charlie.

"I think she looks scared," said Jordan.

"Five deaths in one school year. What do you think happened to them?" Kit asked. They sat quietly for a moment.

"There's only one way to find out," said Jordan. "We have to find Devon Morton." She quickly pulled out her phone and began searching through her e-mails for the article.

She pulled up the article and began reading aloud: "'To place a produce delivery order, visit www.mortonproduce.com.' A website! Kit, can we get on your computer?"

"Are you saying you can't pull that up on your fancy phone?" Kit teased, motioning for them to follow her into the house.

The Morton Produce website was pretty basic: an order form for various vegetables and fruits and a place to fill in the delivery address.

"Go to contact info," Charlie instructed, leaning over Jordan's shoulder. She could feel his breath on her neck.

"This just has the address in Clintsville," she noted as she clicked the link. "No phone number."

"I guess we're going to Clintsville," Charlie declared.

The three squeezed into Charlie's truck, with Jordan in the middle to help Charlie with directions.

"It sure is cozy in here," Kit said under her breath. She gave Jordan a slight jab to the side. Of course, Jordan didn't mind being so close to Charlie. In fact, if she wasn't so anxious about the meeting with Devon Morton, she might have actually enjoyed the strange road trip.

It took them about thirty minutes to get to the Clintsville town limits.

"I guess this is it," Charlie said, looking out the window at mostly empty fields.

They drove a little farther through the main drag of town. There wasn't much there—a bank, a church, a bar. Everything looked kind of run-down to Jordan, like it hadn't been updated since it was built.

They drove slowly, checking the addresses on a few small houses. They passed one with a porch in the front. An elderly couple sat there, rocking slowly back and forth on chairs, staring at them.

"Do you think we should ask them?" Jordan wondered out loud.

"I don't see anyone else to ask," Kit replied. She rolled down her window. "Excuse me. Do you know where we can find Morton Produce?"

The woman remained expressionless as she pointed and said, "Down the road about a quarter mile. Turn off the main road. Drive a little further. There's a red mailbox, says Morton."

"Well, she was creepy," Kit commented after she'd rolled up the window.

They continued in silence, following the

old woman's instructions. When she spotted the red mailbox, Jordan started to feel very nervous.

"Ready?" Charlie asked, looking at her.

"Yes." She smiled slightly. They parked the truck and headed toward a small, old house tucked behind several large trees. There was a larger building farther out.

"That must be where he grows all the hydro beans and super carrots," said Kit.

Jordan took a deep breath as she stepped onto the front stoop and rang the bell. She could hear a rustling inside. Then a man's face appeared behind the screen.

"Can I help you?" he said in a low voice.

"I hope so," replied Jordan truthfully. "We're students from Bridgewater High."

"That's none of my concern," said the man, more gruffly this time, beginning to turn away.

"Please, are you Devon Morton?"

"I am, but I'm not talking to any reporters. Especially kid reporters."

"No, we're not reporters. We're . . . there's been an accident." Jordan could hear the desperation in her own voice. Mr. Morton eyed her for a moment. Then he slowly opened the door to let them in.

"Thank you."

"Sorry, that's Mitch's fault," he commented, motioning for them to take a seat on an old sofa that was covered in a plaid blanket and dog hair. "Why did you come to see me?"

Jordan started. "I saw the yearbook from 1975. I saw your name in the paper. You were friends with those kids who died."

"That was a long time ago," Mr. Morton replied softly.

"Yes, but there's been some accidents this week. Lots of accidents, actually. I think the deaths might have something to do with them."

"What kind of accidents?" Mr. Morton asked.

Jordan, Charlie, and Kit began the long tale of everything that had happened that week. Mr. Morton sat silently, staring at his boots as they described what had happened to Carlos, Thomas, the St. Philomena's student, even the weird incidents in their classes that afternoon. Finally, Jordan brought up what had been bothering her the most. "And there's one other thing. Every time someone gets hurt, there's this . . . sound."

Mr. Morton's head snapped up, and he fixed his eyes on Jordan. "What kind of sound?"

"Wailing," Jordan and Charlie said at the same time.

Mr. Morton buried his head in his hands and began to shake. He mumbled something.

"Sir? Mr. Morton? Are you OK?" Charlie jumped up to help him. "What is it?"

Mr. Morton sat up so they could see his face. Jordan could see tears in his eyes. "Chelsea Knight," he whispered.

He took a deep breath. "A long time ago, when I was about your age, we used to pull pranks on each other. Nothing malicious—it was always just for fun. We'd egg someone's house or put something stupid on their locker. Just kids playing around.

"But one time, some of the kids wanted to mess with this one girl. I'm not sure why—I guess because she was kind of a nerd. She stuttered a little when she talked. She always looked really nervous. I never knew her that well. She was a little younger than me, very small and always alone. Some people said she'd barely talked since her father died.

"Anyway, there was this girl Lizzie. She was really pretty. Fun too. Homecoming queen, a cheerleader. We were all kind of in love with her, I suppose." A small, sad smile crossed Mr. Morton's face.

"Lizzie had it out for the nerdy girl, Chelsea. She thought Chelsea had ratted on her for smoking in the bathroom."

"Did she?" Jordan asked.

Mr. Morton shook his head. "You could never be sure. Lizzie was always doing stuff like that, sneaking off to smoke or skipping class. And she had plenty of enemies—lots of girls she was hard on. Anyone could have ratted on her.

"Anyway. Lizzie had the idea to invite Chelsea to hang out with us after school. Like we'd suddenly decided to become friends with her."

Jordan felt a twinge of empathy for Chelsea. She thought about how she'd felt when Briony had asked her to meet everyone at the Chowder Hut that day after school.

"So we all met up at the roller-skating rink. Chelsea was quiet at first, but after a while she was skating around, laughing. We were all really nice to her. You could tell she was happy to finally have some friends. A few of the guys even couple-skated with her, just to make the whole thing seem more realistic."

"Did you skate with her?" Kit asked.

Mr. Morton shook his head. "I couldn't. I felt bad for her. Even that night while she was having fun, I knew it wouldn't last. Then Lizzie asked her to meet us the next night for a secret séance."

"What's a séance?" Charlie said.

"It's kinda like when a group of people gets together and holds hands," Kit started before Mr. Morton could answer. "They try to combine their energy—to bring out the spirit of a ghost. It seems kinda creepy."

"It is," Mr. Morton agreed. "That night we weren't really trying to attract ghosts. The whole thing was just a hoax—to give Chelsea a scare. We went to this old well on my buddy Gibby's family's farm, in the middle of nowhere. No one would know we were out there.

"Chelsea showed up. I could tell she'd done her hair, taken it out of those braids she always wore. She might have even put on some makeup. Anyway, she looked pretty." Mr. Morton sounded wistful. "She also looked nervous." Mr. Morton's voice sharpened now. "Lizzie told us to join hands. She said we were going to bring out the spirit of Chelsea's dead father. I was next to Chelsea, holding her right hand. I could feel it trembling. Everyone was quiet for a minute. Then Lizzie made a sound—a signal that we should all start to make strange noises, wailing noises, as if we were possessed by some kind of ghost. Lizzie started and all the others followed—everyone except Chelsea and me."

"Why didn't you join in?" Jordan asked.

"I could feel her trembling beside me. Then I heard her start to cry quietly. I could tell she was scared. I thought Lizzie was going too far.

"All of a sudden everyone stopped the wailing. It was silent. Then Lizzie spoke. She said she could hear the voice of Chelsea's father. She said he wanted Chelsea to be lifted to him. We would all lift her up, so he could bless her.

"At this point I wanted the whole thing to be over. It wasn't funny anymore. I told her, 'You don't have to do this,' but she said it was OK. That she would do what they wanted her to.

"I stood back, and they each took one of her wrists or ankles. She was so small. They held her over the well and began wailing again. Then they were swinging her back and forth, faster and faster. She started to cry, really hard this time, and asked to be put down. I begged them to put her down, too, but no one would listen. She tried to wriggle out of their hold. I tried to help grab her away from them, but . . ." Mr. Morton's voice broke. He looked like he wouldn't continue.

"But what?" Jordan cried.

"It was too late. She pulled herself out of their grasp, and they lost control. They dropped her into the well."

That poor, lonely little girl got dropped into a well? Jordan could barely stand the thought of it.

"We could hear her in there for a few minutes. We could hear a wailing sound, not unlike the noise the others were making when they were pretending to talk to ghosts. Then it was silent."

They were all quiet for a moment, taking in what they'd just heard.

"What happened to everyone?" Jordan finally asked.

"Everyone ran scared. No one admitted what had really happened that night. They all said Chelsea was a weird girl, that they'd tried to help her, but she'd jumped in. They said she'd killed herself. I tried to tell the truth, but they outnumbered me. No one believed me.

"A few weeks later they started to show up dead. One right after another. Lizzie electrocuted herself with a curling iron in the bathtub. Ted got in a car accident. Pete slipped on the floor in the locker room and snapped his neck. Gibby hung himself. And every time one of them died . . . someone heard the low wail."

Jordan was speechless.

"For a long time, I thought I'd be next," Mr. Morton continued. "I thought I'd have some freak accident. I even thought maybe I'd just get so sick of feeling like I was going to die— maybe I'd go like Gibby.

"But I guess eventually I just got used to the idea that maybe she didn't want me. She took all the others within a few weeks of each other, but not me. Then you come here and tell me what's going on. You heard the wailing . . . and it's like it's all coming back."

Jordan felt chills. "How come we never heard about this before? My dad won't even talk about it."

"Right after it happened there were all kinds of reporters asking questions. They wanted to write a story about what had happened, but for some reason no stories ever got published. The rumor is that the mayor decided it would be better if everyone forgot it ever happened. I guess the kids' parents and the school agreed. But . . . sometimes I wonder if Chelsea had something to do with it. She didn't want the story of her death hyped up in the media; she was always a private person."

"So, if this Chelsea ghost is haunting us now, what can we do about it?" Jordan asked.

"You have to stop this girl, the ringleader. As long as she keeps up with her games and hurts people, Chelsea will seek revenge." With that, Mr. Morton stood up and pointed toward the door. "It's time you headed out," he said. It was more of a statement than a request.

Jordan looked sorrowfully at the man, knowing she had brought up a lot of things he'd been spending years trying to forget. Jordan wondered if the deaths of her classmates would haunt her in the same way.

Jordan, Charlie, and Kit gathered their things and headed out the door. "Thank you," Jordan said to Mr. Morton as they left.
"Be careful," he replied gravely.

Once they were in the truck, Kit erupted. "So, now we know there's a ghost haunting the school and *everyone* will die! *What* are we supposed to do with that?!" She slammed her fist into the ceiling of Charlie's truck.

"Hey," Charlie muttered, "watch it."

"Hey," Kit shot back, "this is all *your* fault. You and your stupid friends! Now we are all screwed."

Charlie's mouth opened, but he said nothing.

"OK, calm down you guys," Jordan said. "We just need to find a way to stop her, and it all goes away."

"How're we gonna stop a ghost?" Charlie asked, helplessly.

Jordan looked at him for a long moment. "I was talking about Briony," she replied.

Jordan checked the clock—8:30 P.M. She thought for a minute. "We need to get all of Briony's friends together if we're going to stop her. We all started this mess, and we'll finish it. We need to pick up Kevin, and then we're going back to the hospital to see if we can get Carlos, too."

"OK," Charlie replied, taking a deep breath. "Let's do it."

"And drop me off?" Kit said hopefully.

Jordan smiled at her. "Yeah, we've got it from here on out. Thanks for everything."
"Sure. Anytime you need to hunt for ghosts, you know where to find me."

Kevin was wearing sweats and eating pizza when they showed up to get him at his house. They practically had to force him to get dressed and come with them.

When they arrived at the hospital, Carlos was alone in his room, sleeping. Charlie nudged him awake.

"What are you guys doing here again?" he said, rubbing his eyes.

"We've got to talk to you—both of you," Jordan said, looking at Kevin. "We think we know why all this crazy stuff has been going on, but we need your help to stop it."

She took a deep breath and told the story that Devon Morton had told, trying not to forget anything.

"I can't believe it," Carlos said, shaking his head. "You're saying a ghost pushed me off the roof?"

It was Charlie's turn to speak. "There's something else you don't know." As he began to tell the horrible story of Thomas's death, Carlos's face went pale. Charlie talked about the wailing noises they'd heard that night at Judd Powell's house.

When Charlie was finished, Jordan looked around the room expectantly. "So? What do you think?"

"I think you're crazy," Kevin said. "I can't believe you dragged me away from the TV for this."

"C'mon, Kev," Charlie pleaded. "We need to confront Briony together. Maybe if all her friends are there, she'll listen."

Jordan couldn't believe Kevin could just dismiss all of this. "Don't you get it?" she cried.

"This is exactly what is happening to us, all because of Briony's stupid plan. People are dying!"

"OK, I believe you," Carlos said quietly from the hospital bed. "Kev, something happened to me that night. I don't know what it was, but if it was a ghost or whatever, I guess would believe it. There's no way I just fell off that roof. We should listen to Jordan."

Kevin looked baffled. "Are you serious, man?"

"Dead serious. But my parents will freak if I leave the hospital. I need you to represent me while I'm stuck in this bed. Thomas needs you, too."

Kevin sighed and turned to Jordan. "Alright, I'm in. What do you want me to do?"

Jordan smiled with relief. "Just show up tomorrow, wherever Briony tells us to go. And follow my lead."

"**D**o you really want to go to the game after all that's happened?" Jordan's mom said from the doorway.

Jordan nodded. "I think it would be good to show my support. There's been so much tragedy. I'm hoping everyone can come together for this." But the truth was, there would be *more* tragedy if Jordan didn't show up and stop Briony's plan.

"Well, OK then." Jordan's mom looked doubtful.

"Thanks for letting me do this," Jordan said, hearing the beep of Charlie's truck outside. Tears stung her eyes. She wasn't sure if she'd make it back home tonight. Maybe she would be the next one to die. "I love you guys," Jordan said, kissing her mom on the cheek.

"So, where are we going?" Jordan asked as she hopped into the passenger seat.

"Briony said to meet under the bleachers," Charlie said. He looked pale. His fingers fidgeted on the steering wheel.

"Won't people see us?"

"I guess that's why we're going before anyone arrives. Plus, these bleachers have a wall around them. You have to actually go in a door to get under them."

Jordan could felt a familiar sickness in her stomach. She wondered what Briony had planned.

At the field, they walked down to the bleachers. Jordan followed Charlie to a door. Black against a black wall. It would be easy to miss it if you weren't looking for it.

Inside, Kevin was already there with Briony. She sat cross-legged, arranging stacks of fireworks. Jordan hardly recognized her at first. She looked disheveled and wild-eyed. Kevin looked at Charlie and Jordan with fear in his eyes.

"What are you doing, Briony?" Jordan asked.

She smiled maniacally. "I'm getting everything ready for our *fireworks show* tonight!"

"What are you talking about?" Charlie demanded.

"All the players are gonna come out, and they'll start doing the St. Philomena's fight song. Everyone will be on their feet in the home section, singing along. Then all of a sudden, *BAM!* Everyone will panic and run out on the field."

"It'll be like a stampede!" she continued. "They'll trample each other. Then they'll have to forfeit the game. Bridgewater will be the champions!"

Jordan gazed at the massive pile of fireworks. It certainly looked like it could give the crowd a scare, especially with everyone nervous from the last week's deaths. Then it hit her. The fireworks would do more than that—they'd also set fire to the wooden risers above the group, crushing all four of them once the risers collapsed.

"That's not going to happen tonight, Briony," Jordan said calmly as she could. She noticed that Briony already held a matchbook in her hand.

"Of course it's going to happen—with or without you! Tell her, Charlie!"

Charlie took a deep breath. "Briony, we're not doing it. We're not doing these stupid pranks. We're not doing everything you tell us to do."

Briony stared at Charlie, and her mouth twisted into the horrible expression Jordan had seen the day she was nominated for homecoming queen. "Kevin?" she shrieked.

Kevin looked at Jordan and shrugged, unsure what to do. She nodded at him. "Kevin, tell her."

"People are getting hurt," Kevin mumbled at first, but his voice rose. "We can't do this anymore. We have to think about Carlos and Thomas. Thomas is dead, Briony! Don't you get that?"

"Are you guys serious?" Briony shrieked. "You're going to make me do this all by myself!?"

With that, Briony struck a match. She leaned toward a long fuse that led to the pile of fireworks.

Jordan glanced quickly overhead at the wooden risers. *We have to stop her now*, she thought desperately.

"Briony! Don't do it!" Charlie shouted. He stepped toward her but stopped when she flashed an angry grimace and wielded the match at him. The glow created a spooky light around her face. Her eyes looked black.

"Careful!" Jordan warned. "We don't want her to drop the match."

"You don't care about me!" she screamed at Charlie. "None of you ever care about what I want!"

"That's not true," Charlie tried to reason with her.

"Briony!" Jordan yelled, catching Briony's dark eyes. "We took it too far! Nothing good can come of all this . . . hate!"

Briony turned around swiftly. Mumbling to herself, she crouched and lit the fuse. The flame started traveling up the fuse, and Jordan leaped toward Briony. "We have to get out of here!" Jordan shouted. She tried to drag Briony away from the pile. Briony shoved her away with surprising strength. Jordan heard a few loud pops as some of the first fireworks went off.

No! It's too late! Jordan felt Charlie grab her hand. She could no longer see Briony through the billowing smoke.

Then Jordan heard the familiar sound, a low wailing. Out of nowhere the space was filled with cool air. Jordan felt a distinct *whoosh*, and then everything went black.

Jordan blinked for a moment before her eyes adjusted again. Briony was crouched among the still-smoking explosives.

Briony looked at Jordan like she'd never seen her before. Then she looked down at the pile of fireworks surrounding her. All of a sudden, her face fell and she began to cry softly. "Where did all this stuff come from?" She began to stand up slowly. She stared at her filthy hands and grubby jeans in disbelief. "I can't go to the game like this."

It was as if a spell had been broken.

"Yes, you should go home to change for the homecoming parade," Jordan said softly.

Briony looked at Charlie and held out her arm. He took it and began to lead her out of the darkness.

She looked so fragile and confused that Jordan felt a bit sorry for her. She seemed to have no idea of what she'd almost done. She knew Charlie would take Briony home, and they would be dressed up to accept their crowns later that night as if none of this had ever happened. Jordan probably wouldn't hang out with him anymore. *At least we've stopped the madness*, she thought.

As she scooped up the fireworks, she felt a calmness come over her. She felt normal—something she hadn't felt all week. *Kit is never going to believe this*, she thought. She had started to gather them back into their boxes when Charlie appeared again.

"Let me help you with that," he said, taking the fireworks boxes from her arms.

"What are you still doing here?" Jordan asked. "I thought you were taking Briony home and getting ready for tonight."

"Nah, Kevin took her."

"Oh," Jordan smiled, slipping her phone back into her bag

"So what do you think happened here?" Charlie asked, clearly puzzled. "I saw a burst of flames and was sure the bleachers were about to explode. Then everything suddenly went black."

Jordan was surprised. "Didn't you hear that wailing sound? I think it was Chelsea. When we stood up against Briony, it was like the curse was reversed," Jordan told him.

"Chelsea may have helped, but it could never have happened without you, Jordan," Charlie replied.

Jordan blushed and tried to change the subject. "So are you going to stay for the game?"

"Is that what you want to do?"

"Honestly, I hadn't even thought about it," she answered truthfully. "Doing nothing sounds pretty good after this week!"

"That sounds perfect," Charlie smiled. "And after nothing, maybe I can take you to the dance? I mean . . . if you want to go."

She smiled back, nodding, and let him take her hand as they walked away from the field.

Everything's fine in Bridgewater. Really ...

Or is it?

Look for all the titles from the
Night Fall collection.

THE CLUB

Bored after school, Josh and his friends decide to try out an old board game. The group chuckles at Black Magic's promises of good fortune. But when their luck starts skyrocketing—and horror strikes their enemies—the game stops being funny. How can Josh stop what he's unleashed? Answers lie in an old diary—but ending the game may be deadlier than any curse.

THE COMBINATION

Dante only thinks about football. Miranda's worried about applying to college. Neither one wants to worry about a locker combination too. But they'll have to learn their combos fast—if they want to survive. Dante discovers that an insane architect designed St. Philomena High, and he's made the school into a doomsday machine. If too many kids miss their combinations, no one gets out alive.

FOUL

Rhino is one of Bridgewater best basketball players—except when it comes to making free throws. It's not a big deal, until he begins receiving strange threats. If Rhino can't make his shots at the free throw line, someone will start hurting the people around him. Everyone's a suspect: a college recruiter, Rhino's jealous best friend, and the father Rhino never knew—who recently escaped from prison.

LAST DESSERTS

Ella loves to practice designs for the bakery she'll someday own. She's also one of the few people not to try the cookies and cakes made by a mysterious new baker. Soon the people who ate the baker's treats start acting oddly, and Ella wonders if the cookies are to blame. Can her baking skills help her save her best friend—and herself?

THE LATE BUS

Lamar takes the "late bus" home from school after practice each day. After the bus's beloved driver passes away, Lamar begins to see strange things—demonic figures, preparing to attack the bus. Soon he learns the demons are after Mr. Rumble, the freaky new bus driver. Can Lamar rescue his fellow passengers, or will Rumble's past come back to destroy them all?

LOCK-IN

The Fresh Start Lock-In was supposed to bring the students of Bridgewater closer together. Jackie didn't think it would work, but she didn't think she'd have to fight for her life, either. A group of outsider kids who like to play werewolf might not be playing anymore. Will Jackie and her brother escape Bridgewater High before morning? Or will a pack of crazed students take them down?

MESSAGES FROM BEYOND

Some guy named Ethan has been texting Cassie. He seems to know all about her—but she can't place him. Cassie thinks one of her friends is punking her. But she can't ignore how Ethan looks just like the guy in her nightmares. The search for Ethan draws her into a struggle for her life. Will Cassie be able to break free from her mysterious stalker?

THE PRANK

Pranks make Jordan nervous. But when a group of popular kids invite her along on a series of practical jokes, she doesn't turn them down. As the pranks begin to go horribly wrong, Jordan and her crush Charlie work to discover the cause of the accidents. Is the spirit of a prank victim who died twenty years earlier to blame? And can Jordan stop the final prank, or will the haunting continue?

THE PROTECTORS

Luke's life has never been "normal." His mother holds séances and his crazy stepfather works as Bridgewater's mortician. But living in a funeral home never bothered Luke—until his mom's accident. Then the bodies in the funeral home start delivering messages to him, and Luke is certain he's going nuts. When they start offering clues to his mother's death, he has no choice but to listen.

SKIN

It looks like a pizza exploded on Nick Barry's face. But a bad rash is the least of his problems. Something sinister is living underneath Nick's skin. Where did it come from? What does it want? With the help of a dead kid's diary, Nick slowly learns the answers. But there's still one question he must face: how do you destroy an evil that's inside you?

THAW

A storm caused a major power outage in Bridgewater. Now a project at the Institute for Cryogenic Experimentation is ruined, and the thawed-out bodies of twenty-seven federal inmates are missing. At first, Dani didn't think much of the news. Then her best friend Jake disappeared. To get him back, Dani must enter a dangerous alternate reality where a defrosted inmate is beginning to act like a god.

UNTHINKABLE

Omar Phillips is Bridgewater High's favorite local teen author. His Facebook fans can't wait for his next horror story. But lately Omar's imagination has turned against him. Horrifying visions of death and destruction come at him with wide-screen intensity. The only way to stop the visions is to write them down. Until they start coming true . . .

SOUTHSIDE HIGH

ARE YOU A SURVIVOR?

check out all the books in the

SURVIVING SOUTH SIDE

collection.

Bad Deal

Fish hates taking his ADHD meds. They help him concentrate, but they also make him feel weird. When a cute girl needs a boost to study for tests, Fish offers her a pill. Soon more kids want pills, and Fish likes the profits. To keep from running out, Fish finds a doctor who sells phony prescriptions. After the doctor is arrested, Fish decides to tell the truth. But will that cost him his friends?

Beaten

Paige is a cheerleader. Ty's a football star. They seem like the perfect couple. But when they have their first fight, Ty scares Paige with his anger. Then after losing a game, Ty goes ballistic and hits Paige. Ty is arrested for assault, but Paige still secretly meets up with him. What's worse—flinching every time your boyfriend gets angry, or being alone?

Benito Runs

Benito's father has been in Iraq for over a year. When he returns, Benito's family life is not the same. Dad suffers from PTSD—post-traumatic stress disorder—and yells constantly. Benito can't handle seeing his dad so crazy, so he decides to run away. Will Benny find a new life? Or will he learn how to deal with his dad—through good times and bad?

PLAN B

Lucy has her life planned: she'll graduate high school and join her boyfriend at college in Austin. She'll become a Spanish teacher and of course they'll get married. So there's no reason to wait to sleep together, right? They try to be careful, but Lucy gets pregnant. Lucy's plan is gone. How will she make the most difficult decision of her life?

RECRUITED

Kadeem is Southside High's star quarterback. College scouts are seeking him out. One recruiter even introduces him to a college cheerleader and gives him money to have a good time. But then officials start to investigate illegal recruiting. Will Kadeem decide to help their investigation, though it means the end of the good times? What will it do to his chances of playing in college?

Shattered Star

Cassie is the best singer at Southside. She dreams of being famous. Cassie skips school to try out for a national talent competition. But her hopes sink when she sees the line. Then a talent agent shows up and tells Cassie she has "the look" he wants. Soon she is lying and missing glee club rehearsal to meet with him. And he's asking her for more each time. How far will Cassie go for her shot at fame?